Jonny Punkinhead

Jonny Punkinhead

Amy Sterling Casil

ÆGYPAN PRESS

Jonny Punkinhead
A publication of
ÆGYPAN PRESS

www.Aegypan.com

*O*utside my office, I hear the rubbery squeal of a wheelchair, followed by the damp exhalation of a sick child's sigh. The shadow of the pumpkin-headed boy, Jonny, crosses the wall like a dark hand slapped on a sheet.

"Come in," I call through the open door.

"Sure, Dr. Arlan," Jonny says, lisping. It sounds like "sssir, docker awrin," but I'm used to the way he talks.

Jonny wheels into my office. He's very limber with the chair. In his hand is a small, crooked paper Santa and something else that I can't quite fathom, made of festive paper. I finish the letter I'm composing and smile. It's not easy to smile at Jonny.

He holds the paper Santa up. "I made this for gramma," he says.

"That's a great St. Nick," I say. My mouth twists in a funny way, and I don't like the feeling. His grandmother hasn't visited him for at least three years, yet Jonny makes her something for every holiday. Her presents are all in a shoebox, tucked neatly in his cubby in Dorm A., where the seriously ill children live.

"This is for you," he says, holding out the other bit of artwork. I see now that it's pieces of paper, cut and pasted to look like a Christmas present.

The little present has "I love you, Dr. Arlan" written on it in spidery letters. "That's a great job, Jonny."

In a fit of the unprofessionalism which seems to have become my habit of late, I push away from the desk and walk to Jonny's side, then kiss his patchy scalp. Jonny giggles and kisses me back. If I look in his good left eye, which is large, brown, and very pretty, I can pretend for a moment he's a normal child. He turns toward me as he laughs, and it's impossible to pretend any longer.

Jonny's third eye stares vacantly. He can see only from his left eye, not the one on the right or the one in the center of his large, flat forehead. I gently stroke his veined head, which is twice as large as the head of a child his age should be, and I whisper that his grandmother will be very pleased with his gift.

Someone has named the syndrome from which Jonny suffers Webern syndrome. It's not a common birth defect, but it's one of the more unpleasant conditions children have come to suffer from in this, our pestilent age.

I'm Hedrick Arlan, forty-six years old, a doctor of education, not medicine. I've been the administrator of Southern California Sherman Institute for Differently Abled Children for six years. Jonny is nearly seven. He and I arrived at this place on the same day. He is a part of the landscape, like our chairs, molded in solid hunks of indestructible plastic, the mottled gray composite floors, the nurses, the aides, the ever-present medication and the constant stream of visitors who want to gawk at the children.

"Gramma is coming," he says, spraying my face with his spittle. "This year, I know she'll come."

"Of course she will," I say. The lies fall so easily from my lips these days. I pat Jonny's twisted back and watch him wheel slowly from my office, waving goodbye with one tiny six-fingered hand.

Jonny's family signed him over to the state and has forgotten he was ever born. Part of me understands their distress at bearing such a child into the world. Another part of me knows the history and I can't help but feel a nasty stab of fury in my gut, because Jonny's mother drank daily during her pregnancy, and took every drug she could find in staggering quantities.

Was it the drugs that made Jonny what he is? I don't know. They say the virus which altered Jonny's genes is both sly and opportunistic. The thing at work inside of him found a dirty needle somewhere or came through a perforated condom, that much we do know.

When I first came, my friends would ask, "how can you stand all those little children, suffering?" They said this in a disbelieving tone that really meant, "I can't believe you're taking care of those wretches."

Now, they ask less often.

Years ago, Sherman housed developmentally disabled children, the ones they called "morons" and "imbeciles." But no longer. This disease Jonny has, the DNA thief, started a decade ago. The initial wave of the stricken didn't fall ill, so most of them didn't realize that anything was happening, while the tiny bit of protein that saw them as a universe of meat lodged in their gametes, multiplied itself, *changed things*. Then, they bore children. Children with something worse than missing limbs, or hydrocephaly or spina bifida or muscular dystrophy or cerebral palsy.

These children were born with bizarre defects, like Jonny's; a head sized and shaped like a great jack-o-lantern covered with patchy hair, extra fingers, extra toes, a spinal deformity that rendered him paraplegic and the ultimate horror, a blind, filmy, goggling third eye.

Then there were the children with no eyes, merely a nose hole and a gaping maw for a mouth. The children with three arms and a tail, with fishy scales and slit-eyes, the ones with fins in place of hands and feet.

And the horrible irony was that most of Sherman's charges were of normal intelligence. No gravely mentally-disabled among them, these children were born with the ability, though they may not have even had eyes with which to see, of knowing how different they were, and one day perhaps realizing that despite all their pretty names, like "differently-abled," they were what most people called monsters.

I know the histories of our children, save the few found in dumpsters or on some church doorstep. Most are inner city kids, many of them brown or black or golden under their fur or scales. Jonny is black.

On certain nights, when I wake in a sweat at three in the morning and trudge to the patio for a cigarette, because my wife Monique will not allow me to smoke in the house, I wonder if God forgot all these children, while they grew in the womb. Why did he gift them with these deformities, why not merely with old-fashioned spina bifida or muscular dystrophy or retardation or fetal alcohol syndrome?

This virus, it's like Blake's scaly angel of death, coming for the first-born sons of the Egyptians, their parents waking to find their beloved children dead. Blake's angel, drawing his foul gossamer wings over the lintels of all the parents of all the children of Sherman.

It's the poison in our lives leaking out, I think, as I drive home to Monique and my lovely girl Karen, who is fifteen and blossoming and perfect in every way; fierce poison leaching from the evil that is our modern lives, destroying and twisting genes, changing babies into monsters. It's the vile despair of the inner city, the hopelessness, the cruelty, the poverty, writing itself large and making itself manifest, opening itself to the cruel, blind dance of proteins, amino acids.

I've left Sherman, and I'm pulling into the pizza place, to bring home a treat for Karen. We like pizza. Monique is on a diet again, and if I don't bring something home, Karen and I will be stuck with pot pies, and I can't bear the thought of that.

I'm still thinking about Jonny and his absent grandmother as I park. I don't notice the guy in the lurid pink minitruck backing out. He squeals to a stop a few inches from my bumper, gives me the finger and yells something ugly. I ignore him. It's not safe these days, getting into something, even in this bright minimall in my well-to-do neighborhood. The stink of his screeching tires stings my nostrils as I get out of the car. It smells like gunpowder. It smells like death.

*K*aren gobbles a piece of pizza, then kisses me on my cheek, before rushing out the door with one of her friends, Gina or Gia, I can't remember which.

"Cheerleader practice, Dad," she says, by way of explanation.

So, I'm left with Monique, who has settled in with her nail polish and a romance novel. I watch the news until it sickens me, then try to read some mystery novel that Monique had purchased and tired of.

I'd hoped I could talk with Karen about Jonny. Karen had always shown an interest in the children, even when she herself was a young child. She's such a bright girl, so sensitive. But, I thought, she's growing up. She's out more often than in. My friends tell me all teenagers are like this.

Monique's face is porcelain smooth as she reads her book. It's as if nothing has touched her over the years. I've put on more pounds than I care to count. My face is lined, my moustache peppered depressingly with gray, and I wear what we used to charitably call "old man pants," yet Monique looks barely different than the day we married. There's no point in talking to her about Jonny. She doesn't even remember his name.

Monique has closed the book and is filing her nails. "Karen's at cheerleader practice," I say.

She nods and murmurs something. I can't quite hear her.

"Tomorrow the Governor's wife is visiting with some people," I say. I hadn't meant to tell Monique about this, but something is pressing me to talk to her this evening.

Monique puts the nail file down and looks up. "Really?" Her cold blue eyes brighten.

"They're coming at eleven. We've got a musical program planned."

"Oh, I'd love to come! Can I just show up?"

"Sure." I wonder why I haven't said something earlier. Everyone has invited their relatives, at least those who are interested in the Governor's wife. Monique should be there. It would look strange if she wasn't.

"That's so exciting. Why didn't you tell me earlier?" Monique is pouting. Several lifetimes ago, I found that expression fascinating.

"It's been so hectic. I forgot, I guess."

Monique shakes her head. She picks up her book.

"Jonny made another ornament for his grandmother today. He's expecting her for Christmas," I say, then I open my book.

Monique pushes her hair back and smiles. "Hed, what should I wear? Do you think the cream suit, or the red jacket, for Christmas? What do you think the Governor's wife will wear?"

I pretend to read. I think I tell Monique to wear the cream suit, and a holiday pin. It doesn't matter. She'll look fine. She always looks fine. Everyone tells me what a beautiful wife I have. I'm glad she wants to see the Governor's wife. Monique is very lovely. She sits in her high-backed, beautiful chair and the light falls across her face, highlighting its delicate planes and perfect features. Her lips curl in a tiny smile.

I can't imagine ever touching her again.

I'm color-blind. That's why I had so much trouble recognizing Jonny's holiday gift. One of the only colors I can truly see is yellow. Perhaps that's why I love Sherman's auditorium. We painted it in shades of yellow and orange, to mirror the Southern California sun.

Monique walks beside me in her cream suit as I lead the Governor's wife and her entourage on a tour of Sherman.

After the first dorm, the Governor's wife's smile looks forced, as if she'd set her face that way and now couldn't change. She's not a young woman. The lines in her forehead deepen with each child we visit.

A tiny vein in her neck starts throbbing when we visit Dorm B. We see the twins, Kyle and Kieran, getting their daily moisturizing bath. It's important for the boys' skin to be kept moist. Their scales flake away and leave large raw patches without daily treatment.

"Oh, what has happened to them?" the Governor's wife whispers.

"They call it congenital ichthyosis," I tell her. "The skin thickens into scales. The boys also have rudimentary gills."

I pat the attendant's arm. She's a great, dark-skinned woman with a brilliant smile. The twins giggle and squirm. "This is their favorite part of the day," she says, in a voice that echoes her native Venezuela.

The Governor's wife asks the attendant a few questions about the twins. I see pain and horror in her eyes, as the boys smile and coo. "You're pretty," one of the boys says. He's talking to Monique. I turn, and my wife looks as though she's eaten a dried-out lime.

I mutter about how the boys are very affectionate.

"How can you stand it?" Monique whispers through gritted teeth.

I just smile. We say goodbye to the attendant and the twins. It's time for the program. I don't want to be late.

We enter the sunny auditorium. The children have colored butcher-paper banners. Their theme is "What I Want to Be When I Grow Up, Santa." The banners show nurses, doctors and railroad engineers. There are no cartoon characters among them. Sherman's children are blissfully ignorant of violent superheroes and insipid cartoons. The pictures remind me of what we used to draw as children, when we believed that nurses and police officers and fire-fighters were heroes.

The Governor's wife smiles again, a more genuine smile. Jonny's class comes to the stage. He is in the front. They sing "Jingle Bells" and "Hark the Herald Angels Sing." When they get to the chorus of "Hark the Herald Angels," Jonny sings "Glory to the newborn King," in a high, sweet, slightly bubbly voice. The Governor's wife claps. Tears glisten in her eyes.

I reach over and grasp Monique's hand. She purses her lips and draws away.

"Oh, his eyes! What would cause that?" the Governor's wife exclaims.

I tell her the name of his syndrome. She shakes her head. Jonny approaches the microphone. "All I want for Christmas is to give my gramma a kiss," he says. The Governor's wife makes a little choking noise, and puts her hand to her mouth. Monique sits still, beside me. The muscles in her thighs are tight as steel cords.

"Will his family be here for Christmas?" the Governor's wife asks. I shrug. Jonny and his class wheel away, amid the applause of the staff and the teachers and the Governor's wife. Monique claps her delicate hands like a doll someone has wound up and set to performing.

The younger children come on stage. They have prepared a mini-Nutcracker for the Governor's wife.

The Governor's wife asks, "who's that darling girl?"

"Little Gyla," I tell her. Gyla is four, nearly five. She's dressed as a tiny Snow Queen, though under the costume she is covered with soft, silvery fur. Her face is heart-shaped, with a sharp chin and a rosebud mouth, her head covered with short fur, save two tufts above her temples that mimic a puppy's ears.

Monique leans near and whispers, "you've never told me about her."

I shake my head. "No, I suppose I haven't. Gyla is a very happy girl."

"What is the matter with her?" The Governor's wife's eyes are narrow, questioning.

"She's a lycanthrope. It's possible she could bite another child. We may have to isolate her, if her . . ."

"That's horrible! She's really very pretty, in an odd way," Monique says. Her mouth is a tight line. I know what she's thinking. She's thinking, what if Karen had been born like this little girl?

Gyla's parents were poor Mexican people, Indians, from a state they call Michoacan. Her mother worked in the garment district in Los Angeles, before Gyla was born. After a series of foster placements, she came to Sherman. She speaks with the accent of her foster parents, who were also from Mexico.

"She says she wants to be a ballerina," I say to the Governor's wife. I pronounce it as Gyla does, "bayareena."

Tears stream down the cheeks of the Governor's wife, marring her perfectly-powdered complexion, as the program draws to a close. I touch her elbow. She stands and claps beside me, as we all do.

"What can I do for them," she says, as she dabs at her eyes with a tissue. Monique is pressing at her arm, muttering how pleased she was to meet her. "What would they like for Christmas? What would they really like?"

My mind whirls. What would the children like? Would the children like band-aids, to put across their weeping wounds? New bodies? New skin? The removal of excess eyes and digits and limbs? Should we get video toys for the blind children, music disks for those who can't hear? Could the Governor's wife purchase acceptance for them, a society that wouldn't stare?

"Socks," I hear myself say. "The children need warm socks."

The Governor's wife asks how many socks are needed.

I tell her there are one hundred and five children, and it would be nice if each child could have two pair, one white, and one colored. Even the children with fins and flippers can use socks.

The socks are promised before Christmas. The Governor's wife kisses me lightly on the cheek, and her handlers lead her away. As she leaves, I feel a tug at my jacket. I look down, and Jonny is beside me.

"Will you call gramma?" he asks.

I smile down at him. "I'll call her. She's giving you socks for Christmas, Jonny," I say. More lies. So simple. I kiss him atop his sensitive head, which is very warm, and Monique and I leave the auditorium.

Monique serves me coffee on our patio, which is furnished in the style of wrought iron favored in New Orleans. The cup is hot, the coffee steaming, its aroma delicious. Monique makes a magnificent cup of coffee.

"Why did you tell her socks?" she asks as she sits beside me. She has her hair in a sleek ponytail. It makes her look like a young girl.

"They need them," I murmur, as I sip the coffee.

"You need a break. Tell the board you want a week off. Two weeks. Let's get away. Karen can stay with my sister." Monique's expression is serious. She pats my hand. It feels as though she's touched me with a warm mitten.

I pull my hand away. "I can't leave now. The staff is continuing class through Christmas. The kids need me. They haven't got homes or families. Jonny still . . ."

"Jonny be damned! Aren't you worth something, Hed? You can't be his father! I'm sorry for them, but they've got to learn to accept what they've been given. Don't pretend to be their father. It's not helping this Jonny. He needs to know there isn't anyone there for him, there isn't . . ."

"How can you be so vicious!" I slam my coffee cup on the table. Ceramic shards spray across my lap, along with most of the coffee. Monique gasps and backs away. I wipe at the mess with the napkin. The look on her face is terrible. I've frightened her.

"You need some time off, Hed. I mean it," she says, and starts toward the house.

"Wait," I say. She turns. I remember how it was for me, long Christmases ago, waiting at our apartment window for my father. My mother always said, "maybe he'll come." Years and years of it, until at last, I didn't go to the window. And he still didn't come. Perhaps that's why I feel this way about the children. Perhaps this pain is why I can understand their pain. Monique looks at me, questioning.

"I'm sorry," I say. "It's because I spent so much time waiting for my own father."

"You told me what happened," Monique says. Her pale, shiny eyes narrow. "Your mother was too weak to tell the truth, that your father had another family and he'd stopped caring for you. Don't make the same mistake with these kids. I may not know very much about the professional parts of your job, but I do know one thing. Lies always hurt more than the truth. Always." Monique swiftly gathered the ceramic chips and spilled coffee with a napkin before she went back in the house.

"Maybe you're right," I called after her. Monique's unexpected insight disturbed me. Long ago, I had thought that she loved me. But it had been so long since she was there for me, so many little hurts gathered together, that I couldn't remember the way I had once felt. I rested my chin on my cupped hand as I surveyed our pristine yard.

"Tell the boy the truth, Hed," she called from the kitchen window. "And ask for that time off. We need it."

Perhaps I would ask. Jonny's face appeared in the back of my mind, demanding my attention, like a credit card bill I couldn't afford.

I walk beside Jonny as he wheels to his dorm. I've told him that his grandmother won't be coming for Christmas. Snot streams over his upper lip. His third eye rolls aimlessly, the way it always does when he's angry or upset. I feed a steady stream of tissues from my pocket into his left hand as he steers the chair with the other hand.

"I can't believe it, Doctor Arlan," he snuffles. "Why won't she come?"

I keep walking, but the chair slows, then stops. Jonny turns. Now comes the hard part. "I don't know," I say. This isn't a lie. I not only don't know why she won't come, I don't know where the grandmother is. All of our letters and notices came back unopened. Her phone was long ago disconnected.

"I remember her," Jonny says. "She said she loved me. She gave me candy."

Though Jonny hasn't seen his grandmother since he was three years old, I believe that he does remember her. Many of Sherman's children have exceptional memories. "I know she did," I say. "Maybe she's sick, Jonny. Maybe something has happened to her, and we can't get in touch with her, to ask her to come."

"You didn't try! You don't care!" Jonny wheels away, furious. My hand is caught in his wheelchair and a large piece of the skin on the back of my hand leaves with him. I swear softly and put my hand to my mouth, then trot after him. Some of the aides stop and stare. I wave them away as I grab his chair.

"We did try, Jonny. Maybe something has happened to her. You have to understand . . ."

"I don't understand! You just want to keep us here. That's why nobody ever comes, because you're afraid they'll take us away!" Jonny stares at me, his face slick with mucus and tears. His right eye, which is as blind as the one in the middle of his forehead, is cast off, fixed somewhere on the wall. The eye from which he sees gazes darkly, fiercely, at me. I turn away.

"Sometimes people have things happen," I say, my voice sounding as feeble as I feel. "My own father never came to see me at Christmas. I waited for him, time after time, but he never came. I wish someone had been able to tell me not to wait, then, the way I'm telling you now."

"You always lie," Jonny says. "You told me gramma was coming last year, and she didn't come. Now you say she can't come."

His face is full of childish anger and pain. I try to kiss him atop his head, which is lolling forward at an alarming angle, and he pushes me away. My sore hand throbs. He hits me in the ribs and that hurts, too.

"I hate you," he says in a toneless voice. Then he starts down the hall. His wheelchair creaks softly.

I murmur soothing things as I follow him to his dorm. He doesn't respond. His left arm dangles as he manipulates the chair with the other arm. He enters the dorm and slowly, painfully, transfers from the chair to his bed. I watch through the security window. He doesn't cry. Finally, I turn away. I'll remind the aides to give him something special for Christmas, perhaps a drawing set. He enjoys artwork. I'm told his pieces are very colorful, though they all look gray to me.

Monique has done the Christmas tree in silver and white. She's obsessed with the new. I remember my childhood trees. The same little toys, the same fading tinsel, the hundred beloved objects, some paper, others glass or plastic, which my mother and I hung with care. Monique adores glamorous trees, the ones with each brand-new ornament carefully matched. Last year, she informed me that the tree was pink and burgundy. At least, I think, as I sip my egg nog and watch our fake gas log fire, I can tell that this year's tree is silver and white, all the varying shades of the paler portion of the gray scale.

Karen is off at some church program. They're making stockings for poor children. It bothers me that she's gone, and I'm alone again with Monique. How old was Karen, when Monique began decorating the tree? Five, six? Jonny's age. Was that the age when children began to lose their sense of magic, their trust in the love in the world? I swirl the nutmeg atop my egg nog, then swallow the whole sweet mess in one gulp.

I pour myself another egg nog and add a stiff slug of bourbon. The phone rings. I stay in my chair by the tree, staring at the fire. Monique is in the kitchen. She can get it.

I hear her voice. She sounds frightened, or angry. Her face is white as she brings me the phone. "Here," she says, thrusting it at me. The antenna stabs my chest. I adjust it and lift it to my ear.

It's the charge nurse at Sherman. Something terrible has happened. They've called an ambulance.

"I'll come," I say. "I can be there in ten minutes."

"It's Jonny," the nurse says. My heart skips a beat. My foot slips a little on the thick rug as I stand. Monique glares.

"You're not going down, are you?" It's not a question.

"I have to. It's an emergency," I say.

"You're drunk. You can't drive. I'll drive you," she says.

Suddenly, I don't want her with me, her accusing eyes, her porcelain face. I push her aside, grab my keys and I'm out the door. I speed through our quiet neighborhood, and I'm at Sherman within ten minutes. I park crookedly in my spot and run into the building.

The charge nurse greets me. She leads me toward Dorm A.

"I'm sorry, Dr. Arlan," she says. Her voice is breathless, rushed. "We had a new aide on duty. Christmas Eve, you know. All our experienced people have the night off. He came from a place for autistic children."

We're drawing closer to the dorm. Children are crying. Some of them are screaming. Nurses and aides crowd outside the dorm, peering through the security window. The charge nurse calls out a warning, and the crowd parts. We enter the dorm.

"I can't understand why the ambulance isn't here," she says.

Jonny is in his bunk. His leg twitches feebly. I see a huge, dark splash on the wall, his bedding and hair stained the same color. The stain is a rich, deep gray, nearly black, the color of blood.

"What has happened to him? Has someone . . ."

"He was beating his head against the wall. All night long. The attendant let it go on, because he was used to autistic children. He didn't realize what could happen."

"He didn't realize how delicate Jonny was," I whisper. The coppery, sickening smell of blood is everywhere. I push the physician's assistant away from his feeble searches with a stethoscope, and touch Jonny's shoulder. It feels cold. He's bled a tremendous amount, and there is a gaping hole in the side of his head where he must have been hitting the wall. I can see the delicate membrane inside, see where it has torn and the blood and tissue has rushed out. His third eye and the other blind eye stare at me. His one sighted eye faces the bloody bedding.

I want to run, but I keep my hand on his shoulder. "Jonny," I whisper. "Jonny, I'm sorry." Then, someone's strong hand grasps my shoulder. A paramedic. The ambulance has finally arrived.

"Move aside," the paramedic says, then he gets a good look at Jonny and swears under his breath. "Who the hell bashed this kid's head open?" Then, he saw the third eye and looked toward me, questioning.

"Webern syndrome," I tell him. The paramedic's partner brushes by and moves a gurney toward Jonny's bunk. The noise of their radios, their equipment, and their chatter is disorienting.

Someone pushes me in the small of my back. Yet another paramedic. "You need to step aside," he says. I do, and the charge nurse follows. They lift Jonny's tiny body from the bed to the gurney. One of the paramedics grimaces and looks away for a brief moment. Even they're not hardened to boys like Jonny.

"He's not going to make it," I say, to no one in particular.

Then, they're wheeling him through the crying children. The blood spreads across Jonny's bunk like the wing of a huge black crow.

"We need to call the counselors in, for the children. Look at them," I tell the charge nurse. The ones still in bed are agitated, flapping their fins back and forth, kicking their stubby flippered legs. The children who can walk are gathered here and there. I hear some trying to comfort the others. One piping voice says, over and over, that Jonny's going to be okay. Even so, I can't get

the memory of his head, split like an overripe pump-
kin, from my mind.

*A*t seven-thirty, the shifts changed. I'm returning to
my office when someone hands me a portable phone.
Monique is on the line.

"We're not waiting for dinner any longer," she says.
"Karen's very upset."

I hear sobbing in the background. "I can't come
now," I tell her. There is a long silence.

Monique sighs. "I'm giving you two hours. If you're
not home by then, I'm talking Karen to my sister's,
then I'm leaving for Cabo. I may not . . ."

"Jonny's been taken to the hospital," I say, the words
rushing out. "He might die. There's massive trauma."

"There's trauma at home," Monique says. "What can
you do for him? There's no point in staying." Her voice
is icy.

"You don't understand."

"I do understand," she says, very slowly. "You're
killing yourself, Hed." Someone touches my sleeve.
One of the nurses. I hold the phone away. She wants
me to go to another counseling session, then check in
with the children in the dorm. I put the phone back
to my ear, but the line is dead.

There were more counseling sessions. I oriented the
third shift. Then, the hospital called. Jonny was dead.
They had not been able to repair his thin, spongy skull.
Could I notify his family?

The board of directors keeps a small wet bar in their
meeting room. I keep the key. Call his family. I laugh,
bitterly, as I open the doors to the wet bar and pour
myself a scotch and soda. I've brought in plenty of ice,
from the children's ice machine.

The night wears on. More scotches, more sodas, between conferences with the counselors, the psychologist, the new charge nurse. The ice is gone, and my coffee cup is nearly all scotch, just a splash of muddy institutional java. Amid a meeting, I stand awkwardly, mumble something, and rush for the restroom. As I relieve myself, I see my aging belly hanging miserably. It's gray, gray with dark hair on it, as gray as I feel. I slump against the cold enamel wall of the stall for what seems like an eternity, before I finally leave.

Instead of returning to my office, I stumble into the auditorium and sit in one of the folding chairs. They've kept the decorations up, the ones the children made for the Governor's wife. Firemen. Nurses. Doctors. A little train engineer. The fireman held his fire hose between flipper-hands. The nurse had a third eye, very nicely drawn, with long curly lashes.

I stare at the figures, until they split and dance before my drunken eyes. My stomach rebels. I'm afraid I'm going to be sick, and stagger from the auditorium. I avoid Jonny's dorm, and return to my office. I call home. No one answers. There is nothing on the machine. I put my head down, just for a moment, and sleep takes me.

The morning charge nurse wakes me. She has pale hair, braided tightly at the nape of her neck. "A message," she says, flinging a piece of paper on my desk.

The message is from Monique. "We opened presents by ourselves. I've gone to Cabo for a week. Karen is with my sister."

I stare at bit of pink paper. It's Christmas Day, and Monique is gone, my darling Karen is gone. I crumple the message and look at the gray, hard-carpeted floor. My mouth quivers. Something hot and wet hits my hand. I am crying.

As I cry, I hear someone at the door. The nurse again? I can't face her. Her eyes accused me of something, when she left the message. Of what? Killing Jonny? Abandoning my wife and child? The door opens a crack, and I hear a tiny voice, asking to come in.

I sniff back the tears. It's not Jonny, but a little girl. She enters, and touches my leg. Gyla, the little dancer. She has something in her hand.

"I made this, Doctor Arlan," she says. She holds out a pretty white ornament, with my name written on it in silvery glitter. She climbs into my lap.

"Thank you," I say.

"You're crying." She wipes the tears from my cheek with her silver-furred hand. I sigh, and draw her head toward my chest, and stroke her between her tiny pointed ears.

"I'm sad."

"You're sad because of Jonny," she says with a child's simplicity. "We're all sad too, but we think he's happy because he went to heaven."

I nod my head. I can't speak. She nestles against my chest. She is wearing tiny, cheap tennis shoes that look like ballet slippers on her delicate feet.

"I'm going to dance in all the ballets, when I grow up." She gives me a big hug.

Her face is a perfect little heart, with lovely pale eyes and a sweet rosebud mouth. Karen looked like that, when she was this child's age. A perfect angel. Gyla's silvery fur is very beautiful. It shines in the dim light of my office.

Gyla does not need these cheap tennis shoes to dance in, I think. She needs slippers, real toe slippers, with ribbons that lace around the ankle. Not pink, but silver to match her silvery fur.

"I'll get you some real ballerina shoes," I say. I pronounce it "bayareena," as she does. Children deserve their dreams. I shall not break Gyla's dream by telling her she pronounces ballerina incorrectly. I stroke her soft fur, and the nape of her neck. She is almost purring. What a lovely child, my little girl. I feel her heart beating against my chest.

"I'll be a beautiful ballerina, and everyone will love me," she whispers.

"Oh yes, my dear," I say. "Everyone will love you."

Gyla kisses me on my rough cheek, but she seems not to notice the stubble. How easily the lies come. How much like the truth they seem.

Gyla kisses me again, harder. It feels like I've cut myself with a razor. She moves away, and I see something dark on her rosebud mouth. I raise my hand to my cheek, then look at my fingers. I see blood, as dark as Jonny's blood. I put my fingers to my lips. The blood tastes salty and sweet.

"Mustn't do, my love," I say. "Ballerinas don't bite."

Her little brow wrinkles, beneath the fur. She looks at me, wide-eyed. "No?" It is the Spanish no, more question than statement.

I shake my head and hug her once more. "You will have slippers and dresses and tights and everything a little ballerina should have," I say. "Everyone will love you."

She feels like a quivering bird in my arms, as she nestles against me, and I rock her in my lap, crooning a little ballerina song, a song she will like, my little girl, my angel, my dear one.